THIS WALKER BOOK BELONGS TO:

First published 1991
by Walker Books Ltd
87 Vauxhall Walk
London SE11 5HJ

This edition published 1999

4 6 8 10 9 7 5 3

Printed in Hong Kong

British Library Cataloguing in Publication Data
A catalogue record for this book is
available from the British Library.

ISBN 0-7445-6938-9 (hb)
ISBN 0-7445-6375-5 (pb)

# Wheels

SHIRLEY HUGHES

# A TALE OF TROTTER STREET

WALKER BOOKS
AND SUBSIDIARIES
LONDON • BOSTON • SYDNEY

Spring at last! The Easter holidays had arrived and the wheels were out on Trotter Street. Sanjit Lal zipped along on his roller-skates, wearing a smart crash-helmet. Little Pete Patterson rode his red tricycle, ring-a-ding-dinging the bell to let everyone know he was coming.

Harvey and Barney took turns on Barney's skateboard and Mae pushed her baby sister Holly in a brand new buggy. Some of the big girls and boys had wonderful, new full-size bikes, even racers! They gathered at the corner to show them off. Carlos and Billy had their old bikes.

Billy's mum looked after Carlos in the school holidays, while *his* mum was at work. When she took Billy's baby brother to the park in the afternoon, Carlos and Billy came too and brought their bikes. They were not old enough to ride on the road, of course. It was too dangerous.

The park was the best place to ride. There was a smooth, wide path which went round the play area then into a steep slope. You could whizz down it, cornering at high speed, and free-wheel the rest of the way, past the old band-stand until, braking gently, you ended up at the bottom by the lake where the ducks swam.

The little kids playing and the mums chatting on the benches and the old lady who came to feed the birds all stopped what they were doing and stared as Carlos and Billy flew past. Whooosh!

There was a narrow, humpbacked bridge over the lake. Carlos and Billy thought it was exciting to race their bikes up one side and down the other. Sometimes Carlos won and sometimes Billy. But if Mr Low, the park-keeper, saw them, he soon put a stop to it. He was very strict about people behaving well in his park. Mr Low did not seem to like fast riding at all, not even on the paths.

Orville, his assistant, was not quite so strict. Sometimes, when Mr Low went off to have a cup of tea in his hut, Orville would call out encouraging things to Carlos and Billy as they raced by.

All the same, Carlos and Billy both wished they had better bikes.

"You can get up a lot more speed on a big bike," said Billy. "They have gears too."

"I've seen one I like in a shop," said Carlos. "Blue and silver with a pump to match."

"I'm going to ask for a new bike for my birthday," said Billy. "It's very soon now."

"It's my birthday soon as well," said Carlos, "and I'm going to get a new bike too."

Carlos asked his mum about this. He had asked her before and he asked her again that evening. But his mum said that new bikes were very expensive. She explained that it was difficult for her to save up for things like bikes. She worked in a bakery and often brought home nice fruit cake and cream buns for Carlos and his big brother Marco – but not very much money.

"Marco's got a proper bike," moaned Carlos.

"He's older than you," said Mum, "and he needs it for his Saturday job. He's saving up for a new mountain-bike. When you're bigger, you can learn to ride his old one."

"But I need a new bike *now*," Carlos said.

Mum only answered: "We'll have to see…"

On the afternoon of his birthday, Billy proudly brought his brand new bike to the park. It was orange, with shiny silver handlebars. Everyone gathered round to admire it. Even Orville left his work to come and have a look.

"Race you!" Billy called out to Carlos, as he pulled away and glided off down the path.

It was not much of a race. Billy won easily. Carlos felt silly pedalling furiously behind, crouched over the handlebars of his old bike. His legs felt too long and his knees kept getting in the way.

After a while Billy's mum suggested that Billy should give Carlos a turn on his new bike, which he very kindly did.

But when Carlos had swooped down the hill like a bird once or twice, he had to give the beautiful bike back to Billy.

In the end, Carlos gave up wanting to race. There was no point.
He threw down his old bike by the lake and sat by himself, tossing
pebbles into the water.

He felt cross with Billy. He even felt cross with the ducks who came swimming over to see if he had any bread.

"You wait! You wait till it's my birthday!" he told them.

On the evening before his birthday, Carlos kept wondering if Mum had managed to get him a bike. He thought she could have hidden one in the shed behind their block of flats.

He even secretly slipped out and tried the shed door, but it was  locked. Was there a bike inside? He looked through a crack, but  he couldn't see anything. Mum had promised that tomorrow she would bring home a very special cake from the shop – a birthday cake for Carlos! She said that he could ask Billy round for tea. But Carlos didn't want Billy to come to his birthday tea.

In bed that night, Carlos was too excited to sleep.

He kept imagining getting a new bike: a big bike, a blue and
silver bike, a bike that was even better and faster than Billy's,
which he could show off in the park. He crept to the window
and looked down at the shed. There was a light on in there!
He could see it shining up through the skylight in the roof.
He watched for a long time. Then he went back to bed.

In the morning, Mum gave
Carlos a big birthday hug.
Marco had gone off early,
but he had left a card
on the kitchen table
with some bears in a
spaceship and "Happy
Birthday, Carlos" written
inside it. There were some

parcels on the table too, all wrapped in fancy paper.

"Aren't you going to open them?" asked Mum, beaming.

Carlos pulled off the papers one by one. There was a jigsaw
puzzle, a new jacket in dazzling red and green, just like the ones
the big boy bikers wore, and a toy car with remote control.
Carlos had wanted one ever since he had seen them in a shop
and he was very pleased. But he knew at once that there was
no new bike.

"Marco's going to give you his present when he comes in at teatime," Mum told him.

Carlos knew that Marco's present could not possibly be a new bike. He would not have nearly enough money for that. Inside, Carlos could not help feeling bitterly disappointed.

When Mum asked him if he would like to go and play with Billy that morning and show him his new things, Carlos said no – he would rather go to the shop with Mum. So he took his new car and played with it in the back of the bakery while his mum served the customers. The car went very well. Everyone made a great fuss of Carlos when they heard it was his birthday. One lady bought him a chocolate cream cake and another gave him some money for his piggy-bank.

When they got home, Mum opened a box and brought out a truly wonderful cake. It was pink and white and covered in icing shells and swirls, with silver holders for the candles. There was a plate of fancy pastries too, and ice-cream. Carlos ate a lot of everything. But when the time came to light his candles, he missed having Billy to help him blow them out.

Then Marco walked in.
He got hold of Carlos and
swung him round, singing
"Happy Birthday to you!"
Then he ate a very large
slice of cake.

"Want to find out what
I've got for you?" said
Marco. "Follow me."

Carlos followed Marco
downstairs. All the way
down, Carlos was
wondering what Marco
was going to give him.

He knew it could not be a bike. So what was it? They walked right
past the shed. Then at last Carlos saw his present!

It was a go-cart! A real go-cart! It had proper steering and rubber wheels and a seat, and it was painted bright red. Marco had made it himself. Carlos was too surprised to speak. Never, ever, in his

wildest dreams had he imagined owning a go-cart! He looked at it for a long time. He stroked its wheels and its little seat. Then he put his head against Marco's arm. "Thanks, Marco," he said.

It was the last day of the holidays. Most of Trotter Street had
turned up in the park for the big event: the Non-Bicycle Race!
The starters were already lined up – Sanjit, Sam, and Ruby Roberts
were on roller-skates; Harvey and Barney had skateboards.

Jim Zolinski and Brains Barrington were in their box-on-wheels;
Frankie had borrowed a scooter, and Mae and Debbie had one
roller-skate each. Carlos was at the controls of his new go-cart,
with Billy crouching behind him. Now Josie lifted the starter's flag…

Ready, steady, GO! Cheering mums, dads and toddlers lined the track. The Bird Lady was there and Orville too. Even Mr Low popped his head round the door of his hut to watch, though mostly to keep an eye on his flower-beds.

Past the play area, into the steep slope, gaining speed then cornering wildly, sometimes crashing but managing to scramble on again, weaving, coasting, trundling they went – all the way down to the lake.

And who came first? Carlos and Billy in the wonderful go-cart, of course!

# MORE WALKER PAPERBACKS
## For You to Enjoy

## Also by Shirley Hughes

### ANGEL MAE

Mae Morgan is delighted to be given the part of the Angel Gabriel
in the school nativity play. But the Morgan family is soon to have a birth of its own.
Will the new baby steal Mae's glory?

"One of Shirley Hughes' best ever picture books… Ideal for three to seven-year-olds."
*Tony Bradman, Parents*

0-7445-2032-0    £4.99

### THE BIG CONCRETE LORRY

The Pattersons' house is so jam-packed with things that
there's hardly room for the Pattersons themselves! But building an extension
is no easy matter, even with the neighbours' help – and especially
when the concrete is the quick-setting kind!

"Shirley Hughes excels at making the ordinary special…
Beautifully crafted." *Books for Keeps*

0-7445-6378-X    £4.99

### THE SNOW LADY

The children on Trotter Street think old Mrs Dean is mean.
When she goes away on Christmas Eve, Sam makes an unflattering snow replica. But then
Mrs Dean returns and Sam worries about hurting her feelings…

"Excellent and recommended for 4 – 7 year-olds and all their families."
*Books for Keeps*

0-7445-2357-5    £4.99

Walker Paperbacks are available from most booksellers, or by post from B.B.C.S., P.O. Box 941, Hull, North Humberside HU1 3YQ
24 hour telephone credit card line 01482 224626

To order, send: Title, author, ISBN number and price for each book ordered, your full name and address,
cheque or postal order payable to BBCS for the total amount and allow the following for postage and packing:
UK and BFPO: £1.00 for the first book, and 50p for each additional book to a maximum of £3.50.
Overseas and Eire: £2.00 for the first book, £1.00 for the second and 50p for each additional book.

Prices and availability are subject to change without notice.